SCARY SHORT STORIES FOR TEENS
BOOK 3

A COLLECTION OF BONE CHILLING, CREEPY, HORROR SHORT STORIES

BRYCE NEALHAM

Copyright © by Bryce Nealham.

All Right Reserved.

No part of this publication may be reproduced, distributed, or transmitted in any form or by any means, including photocopying, recording, or other electronic or mechanical methods, or by any information storage and retrieval system without the prior written permission of the publisher, except in the case of very brief quotations embodied in critical reviews and certain other noncommercial uses permitted by copyright law.

CONTENTS

STORY 1 1
   SUZY DOLL ....
STORY 2 7
   IN THE ATTIC ....
STORY 3 11
   THE PARK ....
STORY 4 15
   HANDSOME DEVIL ....
STORY 5 19
   NOT ALONE IN THE CLOSET ....
STORY 6 23
   THE SPOOKY SUBWAY ....
STORY 7 27
   THEY MOVE ON THEIR OWN ....
STORY 8 31
   GRINNING REVENGE ....
STORY 9 35
   BATH TIME HORROR ....

Story 1

Suzy Doll

My experience all began before I was born. In fact, this isn't really MY story; it's my aunt's. This is a story my aunt had told me many years ago when I was a child.

It was a story I always teased her about and laughed off as nothing more than a fable…but now I know that is not the case.

I am British, born and raised in the north of England. I am not superstitious nor am I religious in any way. I'm telling you this so you understand that I was raised as an atheist and was very skeptical even as a child.

Unfortunately for me, events would take place that would leave me questioning my own beliefs and wondering if my aunt's stories were all real.

It all started when my aunt was around eight or nine years old. It was Christmas Day in the early 70s and she was ripping open her last remaining present. To her surprise and delight it was a doll, but not just any doll, it was the doll she had seen in town months ago and had begged her mother to buy.

She had been devastated when my grandmother refused to buy the doll not realizing she had actually already purchased the doll and it was secretly stashed away in the loft ready for Christmas.

Now, as a young child, she was staring down into the doll's plastic eyes and blonde hair. This doll was the one thing my aunt had wanted above all else.

As she pulled the doll from its package in the blink of an eye she hugged it and exclaimed that it was the greatest present she had ever wanted and that they would be best friends forever. She named it Suzy.

Being similar in size to my aunt, the doll was the perfect best friend. My aunt would spend hours talking to and dressing Suzy in clothes my aunt had just grown out of. Yes, Suzy was not a small doll.

My aunt would scribble on the dolls face with crown to imitate makeup, she would host tea parties and Suzy would be the star attraction.

My aunt would spend hours having one-sided conversations with Suzy as most little girls do with their dolls. Everything seemed completely normal.

My grandparents and my dad never once suspected my aunt was in any danger...but they were wrong.

One night my aunt found herself awake when everyone else in the house was asleep. There was nothing special about the night, nothing in particular had woke her up, she was just simply awake. Climbing from her bed, my aunt still partially asleep, staggered out of her room and began walking downstairs for a glass of water.

She was halfway down the stairs when she heard movement above. Looking up she saw glances of movement scurrying by the stairs banister. Following the movement with her eyes her heart almost stopped.

When she traced the motion to the top of the stairs her blood ran cold and she couldn't speak. The sight before her was so confusing and terrifying that it had stolen her ability to form words.

Standing there at the top of the stairs was her doll Suzy. But that couldn't be! She had left the doll at the bottom of her bed. How could she possibly be standing there at the top of the stairs?

Surely this was every little girls dream for her doll to come to life…right? Sadly, that momentary naiveté and childlike whimsy disappeared as she stared longer at the doll.

Darkness folded around the dolls features and the top of the stairs grew darker and darker as if a cloud hung over it. Suzy's crown stained face was different in the shadows. There was a new sinister intent behind Suzy's lifeless plastic eyes and an insidious look upon her face that filled my aunt with dread.
 Even as a child she had enough instinct to back away a bit. She prayed that this was just some awful dream, some awful nightmare but before she could even attempt to wake herself up the unthinkable happened.

A voice called out from the top of the stairs…the voice of a small girl or something attempting to mimic a little girl. The voice came from her doll Suzy; a doll that had no ability to talk at all.

"Come and play", the voice called out.

When she heard that creepy voice my aunt's whole body began to shake. She could literally feel herself turning white. She had never felt such a feeling before or since that could compare to that reality shattering dread.

She wanted to scream but that the inconceivable was happening to her and her sheer shock was too overwhelming. She could do nothing other than stand there shaking.

Then the doll called to her once more, even raising one of her arms up slowly causing her plastic limbs to grind together and let out a spine-chilling creak.

My aunt let out a silent scream as she felt faint and collapsed on the floor. She lay at the bottom of the step with the darkness encroaching her sight. The final thing she caught a glimpse of was Suzy running back to her room.

The following morning my grandfather found my aunt at the bottom of the steps cold and terrified. She recounted her tale to my grandparents but they never believed her.

Who would believe such a story from a child? There was no way they would accept that a doll had sprung to life. My grandparents told my aunt that she must have been dreaming or sleepwalking.

In any case, my aunt was so terrified by the event that she forced my grandparents to get rid of Suzy.

I know from the outside looking in it must have seemed odd because the doll hadn't actually expressed any desire to hurt her or made any attempt to do so, but my aunt swears that something or someone else was there with the doll speaking through her.

She mentioned that the look on Suzy's plastic face was not a friendly or warming one…it was threatening and terrifying.

My grandmother was devastated that my aunt had become so terrified of the doll; after all it was an expensive gift. However, my grandparents decided it would be best to get rid of Suzy like my aunt wanted.

The problem is, instead of just tossing the doll out they decided to stored it in the loft. This should have been the end of it but of course it wasn't.
 For years my aunt claimed she had heard footsteps pacing along the wooden beams in the loft and even told me she heard voices, nursery rhymes and crying all coming from the loft.

One of the final nights she could recall activity occurring, she was entering her bedroom and as she did she passed under the loft hatch. Just before she closed her bedroom door behind her she heard the voice of a small child whisper.

"Let me out", the voice called down from the loft.

My aunt immediately looked up and noticed the loft hatch quickly shut, suggesting someone had briefly pulled it open to whisper down to her.

This was impossible, it could not have happened because the bolts that kept the hatch shut were on the outside.

Strangely, after that happened, the activity just stopped of its own accord. My aunt grew up, moved out and chalked the experience up to a night terror and an overactive imagination.

My aunt tells me that the doll, Suzy is still up there in the loft. I might just go up there one day and take a look for myself. I mean, this is just a silly story…right?

SCARY SHORT STORIES FOR TEENS - Book 3

STORY 2

IN THE ATTIC

I needed a place to live as I just split up with my girlfriend and so I had to move out of her place. My friend Paul told me he knew of someone who owned a house and that he was renting it out.

The guy's name was Dean and he said I could stay in his place until I found my own apartment. I didn't really have much of a choice so I decided to move into the house.

I arrived at the house and Dean showed me around. The place was nice enough with lots of space and a nice front garden. It was also close to where I work.

As I was looking around I noticed there was a padlock on the hatch to the attic. When I asked him what was up there he just told me there's nothing important up there, just some personal belongings.

I didn't think anything of it at the time. I didn't really blame him for keeping his possessions locked away as I was a total stranger in his home.

My first night there I woke up and around 2:00 a.m. to use the bathroom. After doing my business I headed back to my bedroom when I heard a noise coming from the attic. It sounded like something was being dragged across the floor.

I thought it was just the wind or the house making noises, which happen sometimes. The next night I heard the same noise coming from the attic again, this time waking me up. I sat up and concentrated on the noise. I couldn't figure out what it was. I thought maybe it was rats or something. There wasn't much I could do anyway as the attic was locked shut.

The next day I decided to text Dean and ask him about what could be making the noises in his attic. He just replied by saying it was nothing…probably just a bird that got in there or something.

Every night for the next week I could hear the same noises coming from up there and it woke me up once too many times.

One night I had enough and decided to investigate. I got some bolt cutters and I cut the attic padlock off. I pulled the ladder down and headed up there.

It was really dark, I couldn't see a thing so I went back down to get my phone. I climbed back up the ladder and turned on the torch feature on my phone.

I shone the light around the Attic space. I couldn't really see much, mostly boxes and a few pieces of sports equipment.

As I was searching around I tripped over some boxes knocking them on the floor; some photos fell out. I picked up the photos and took a look at them.

One of the photos was of a woman who was tied to a wall. Her shirt was ripped and she had a bloodied pig mask covering her face.

I was taken aback but I continued to sift through the other photos. Most of them were very similar; with a half-naked women standing or sitting, tied up and wearing a pig mask.

Near the end of the pile of photos I came across another one that showed someone next to the woman. It was Dean and he was holding a large knife up against this woman's throat.

By the way the photo was taken I could tell that he had taken it, selfie style.

The woman didn't have the mask on this time. It looked like she was in pain and was definitely crying because her face was smeared with mascara and what looked like dried blood.

I sifted to the next photo and it was the same woman screaming as Dean seemed to be digging that long knife into her cheek.

Dean had a huge grin on his face...an evil grin.

I couldn't believe what I was seeing and my heart started racing. As I scrambled through the photos looking at more and more of these women being tortured by Dean I felt sick to my stomach and wanted to throw up.

The images were like something you would see in a horror movie. Dean was taking selfie photos while he tortured what looked like multiple women.

There was blood...so much blood.

I was about to head down the ladder to call the police when I heard a noise from across the attic. It was the same noise that's been waking me up every single night.

I slowly wandered over to where the noise was coming from. I saw a blanket and it was covering something up. I pulled the blanket back and almost jumped out of my skin.

I fell down to the ground in shock because right there before me was a woman. She was gagged and chained to the floor. There was dried blood everywhere around her.

She was in her underwear, had bruises and cuts on her body, and a swollen beaten up face.

I carefully pulled the gag off her mouth. She couldn't speak; she was in obvious shock.

I cut her free with the bolt cutters and carried her down to safety. She was very weak and could barely walk. She must have been very dehydrated and probably hungry too.

I quickly called the police and the ambulance right away. When they arrived I told them everything I knew.

It didn't take them long to find Dean to arrest him. It turns out that the poor woman in the attic was actually reported missing about six weeks ago.

Dean was sentenced and charged with kidnapping, torture, false imprisonment and a slew of other things. Weeks later I heard that the woman made a full recovery…physically at least.

STORY 3

THE PARK

This happened to me a few years ago. I was in high school at the time and I would usually get home by going through the local park not too far away.

It probably took longer for me to get home this way but the alternative was a narrow sidewalk next to a busy road. At least going through the park was peaceful and I would occasionally bump into some friends on the way.

On this particular night, however, the park seemed a lot emptier than usual. Not that I minded walking alone given that the area was relatively safe and nothing dangerous or even remotely interesting ever really happened around here.

As I arrived halfway through the park, I noticed something rather strange. Someone had left some of their things on one of the park benches.

At first, I thought it was just some trash that someone hadn't bothered to throw away, but as I got closer, I could see that they were in fact belongings, some of which were valuable.

Despite what I said about the area being safe, it still seemed like a pretty bad idea to leave things out in the open.

My initial conclusion was that perhaps a dog escaped from its leash and the owner ran after it, so I decided to adopt a sense of civic duty by sticking around for a while until someone showed up.

After waiting for at least 15 minutes, I started to wonder if anyone was going to show up that night. Come to think of it, I hadn't seen another soul since I entered the park.

I decided that I had already waited long enough and it was getting quite late. I thought about taking the belongings with me but I didn't want it to look like I was stealing so I just ignored it and moved on.

Then, just as I started walking, I heard something run past me. I heard it again just moments later and it seemed even louder this time around.

Something didn't feel right and for whatever reason, I just started walking away very fast. I felt instantly relieved as I approached the end of the park but this feeling turned out to be extremely short-lived as I noticed a large shadow blocking the way to the exit.

The vague silhouette suggested large animal features that seemed almost predatory in nature and I instantly felt threatened by its appearance.

It stared back at me with its large eyes as if it were trying to anticipate my next move yet remained surprisingly still and silent.

I wasn't very keen on the idea of closing any more distance between myself and whatever it was that stood in my way and given an inherent fear of the unknown, I decided to turn around and quickly head back the same way I came.

I refrained from running but only because I thought doing so may provoke it to start chasing after me.

My heart was pounding but I tried to stay calm as I cautiously made my way back. I didn't want to reveal that I was afraid but I found myself counting every step forward hoping that I wasn't being followed.

I couldn't even bear to look behind me at this point but it was only moments later when I realized I didn't need to. The same dark silhouette appeared once again blocking the path ahead of me, this time, considerably closer.

I slowly backed away without breaking any eye contact with the creature. It seemed content to let me go as I continued to back up further and further away, which is when I discovered the true horror of the situation.

I was being stalked, not by one, but two creatures that were blocking my only means of escape. There was no other way out.

Like hungry sharks, they began to circle around me, slowly closing in for the kill. Then suddenly, I heard something in the distance, followed by small subtle impacts on the ground around me.

The sound of the rain appeared to startle them and they soon ran for cover as it continued to get stronger.

I never thought I would be so happy to catch the rain that day and I was relieved to get home safely.

STORY 4

HANDSOME DEVIL

This happened when I was in college. I was 20 at the time studying for an upcoming exam in biology that is until my roommate burst into my room.

She did that all the time…it was annoying. She wasn't yelling, but I could see she was drunk by her excitement. I completely lost focus on my studies, but it was okay, I kind of got used to her behavior.

She was a party girl while I was more of a nerd. I tried to get back on my reading tracks again but she patted me on the back and drunkenly giggled.

"Come on Rachel, every time I see you you're always reading a book", she said drunkenly.

I sighed, "Every time you come in here you always smell of alcohol and vomit".

She frowned at me. "How about this, I'll be quiet all week if you come to this party tomorrow at 8:00?"

I wanted to say no but then I thought about it…I mean, I do always work really hard. Besides, she won't barge in like this for the whole week! Sounds too good I thought to myself, so I nodded and continued to read.

On the night of the party we got ready. I hadn't dressed up in ages so I was kind of excited.

When we got to the party it was loud and filled with drunken people making out, bumping and dancing. the party was hosted in a basement like setting only it was much bigger and had a lot of space.

I'm not going to lie, I did have a few drinks. I wasn't drunk but I was definitely tipsy. So as my view became tilted this guy comes out of nowhere and starts to talk to me.

I was a little surprised but he was fairly attractive. He didn't seem drunk like all the other guys at the party.

We exchanged names and from what I remember he had red dyed hair and blue eyes. He had an athletic build and was around six feet tall. His name was Ray.

We laughed and talked about topics like studying and books and that kind of thing. The talking went on for about a half an hour.

He then said, "Hey, I'm going to get another drink, do you want anything?"

I said, "Sure". I mean, I'm having fun so why not have another drink?

So, he came back with the drinks and the next thing I remember we were making out in the corner of the party room. It was so quick!

After our kiss he said, "Do you want to come back to my place?"

I politely declined. At this point I already know what he wants, besides I needed to be on campus in the morning.

"Come on, I promise it'll be fun", he said with an innocent smile.

I remember that he kept on trying to get me to go but I kept refusing. He gave up after I made it clear I wasn't interested in going to his place in a much firmer manner.

He rolled his eyes angrily and gave me a paper with a number on it. "Fine...if you change your mind give me a call". He then stood up and walked out of the party room.

The next day I woke up inside my college bedroom on my bed next to my roommate snoring on her bed. As I got up to shower a paper fell out of my pocket, it was the number Ray gave me.

That brought back some memories of the night before but I had more important things to do right now than reminisce. I showered and then sat at my desk to study.

I remember reading my book when all of a sudden I felt dizzy. Next thing I remember is waking up in the bed with police officers and nurses talking next to me.

It turns out I have this dangerous allergic reaction that can only be caused from saliva or any bodily fluids that had come from decaying or rotting flesh.

I was surprised to hear that. I hadn't kissed anyone today let alone ate anything raw. Then I remembered Ray from the night before. I told the police about him and gave them the number he gave me.

I quickly recovered and a few weeks passed after leaving the hospital. I just finished a school test when my phone rang. It was the police.

It turns out the guy from the party, Ray had two dead decaying women's bodies inside his apartment. They must have been there for weeks. He had been feeding off of them. Yes, he ate dead bodies.

I suddenly felt sick…knowing that I made out with someone who ate human flesh. Even worse, what would have happened if I agreed to go to his place?!

STORY 5

NOT ALONE IN THE CLOSET

When I was a kid my parents would sometimes bring me down to my aunt and uncle's place to stay for the weekend. Most of the time, I'd play with my two cousins who were around the same age as me.

My cousins lived on a small farm with plenty of open space and we could run around doing pretty much whatever we wanted if we thought we could get away with it.

The three of us would sometimes cross over to the neighboring farm about half a mile away. It had been abandoned for decades with a scattering of derelict buildings and other structures still standing on the property just begging to be explored.

This was of course a gold mine for three adventurous young boys such as ourselves, especially after my cousins told me stories about the deaths that took place in the house.

It was pretty classic fair; man goes crazy, axe murders his entire family, hangs himself and returns every night as an angry spirit looking for new victims. Yeah, it's good grisly stuff.

Even at that young age I knew they were probably making it up or at least embellishing old rumors. However, seeing as how the setting lent itself so well to such tales I allowed myself to buy into it.

One afternoon we decided to play hide and seek. When it was my turn to hide I ran off for a flimsy brown barn that had living quarters on top.

I climbed the stairs looking for a good spot. There was still furniture inside and personal belongings lay scattered across the floor. I maneuvered over broken dishes, tattered clothes and crumbling books eventually coming to a small room with a closet. Jackpot!

In the closet there were long black dresses still hanging on the rod that I could hide behind. I stepped inside and managed to force shut the folding door. My only illumination was a slit of sunlight that shone through the crack in the door from a nearby window.

I crouched down with knees tucked into my chest and waited to see if my cousins will find me. Some time passed and there was still no sign of my seekers so I waited some more.

Debating if and when I should give myself up after nearly an hour this was starting to get boring. My head drooped and I slowly fell asleep.

I woke up suddenly. It was pitch black. Drowsy and confused I forgot for a minute where I was or what I had been doing. As it came back to me, the realization that it was now nighttime and that I had been abandoned here filled me with sinking dread in the pit of my stomach.

I tried to get up but a sudden cramp in my calf kept me grounded. I squirmed about waiting for it to pass when I heard a door slamming shut downstairs and instantly froze.

There was a brief period of silence and then I heard footsteps at the bottom of the stairs. These were not ordinary steps. I heard one step and then a thud as though someone had a walking stick…or a wooden leg.

These weren't the footfalls of a child. These weren't the footfalls of my cousins. They were slow, heavy and deliberate.

I held my breath praying they would go away…but they did not. The footsteps continued to ascend. After another moment of silence the walking resumed this time along with a steady scraping sound like something heavy being dragged across the floorboards.

The footsteps made their way through the debris and wandered aimlessly through the various rooms. I thought I could smell something faintly putrid.

The constant scrape sent cold shivers coursing down my arms and back. My worst fears were realized when the steps reached the bedroom doorway. They got closer and closer and finally stopped directly in front of the closet door.

I couldn't see a thing. After an agonizing pause they continued on over to the other side of the room and out the doorway again. The footsteps faded away down the hallway.

I waited for what seemed like an eternity until I heard no more sounds. I was trying to build up enough courage to open the door and flee.

Then, three things happened simultaneously. I was bombarded with a smell I can only describe as fresh road kill. I then heard raspy breathing behind me in the dark closet and I felt hot breath against the nape of my neck.

That was enough for me to hurtle myself out from the confines of that nightmare space relying on memory and scant moonlight to navigate through the darkened house.

All the while I heard footsteps chasing behind me closing in with terrifying speed. It was a clumsy, torturous escape full of trips and bumps and blind stumbling. I never looked back at least not until I had burst out the front door and into the country night.

When I did finally look back I saw absolutely nothing. There were no more footsteps and nobody was chasing me. That didn't stop me from running all the way back to my aunt and uncle's house.

There was a police car in the driveway when I got back. My parents were there too, worried sick. Everybody demanded to know where I had been because apparently when my cousins still hadn't found me by evening they'd returned home to tell their parents.

Eventually the police were called in and informed me that they had already scoured every building on the farm. The insinuation that I was lying about my whereabouts didn't go unnoticed. None of it made any sense.

It wasn't until years later that one of my cousin's filled in a final piece of the story. Apparently, when the incident occurred, he and his brothers had spent hours searching for me but the part they didn't tell anyone was that they thought they spotted me in the window of the bedroom I was hiding in.

When they got closer they saw that it wasn't me but instead another young boy.

Neither of them knew who the boy or had ever seen him in school or around town. However, they did notice that he was smiling and waving down at them.

He was gesturing for them to come upstairs. That's when they ran back home…all this while I slept in that dark closet.

Story 6

The Spooky Subway

So this is a creepy story that I don't usually talk about. It happened to me quite a while ago so I probably won't remember all of the details.

However, I will never forget the strange experience that took place at a nearby subway station which drove a sinister wedge between me, my friends and my family.

I was around 19 years of age at the time and I had just started taking music lessons in the evenings. I was at a stage where I was still trying to figure things out and get used to life in the big city.

I remember that the lesson finished a lot later than usual that day for some reason so it was already well past 11 at night by the time I got to the subway which meant that the circulation of trains was few and far between.

As I anxiously waited for the signature sound of a distant train, I observed the platform and was surprised to see how abandoned it was.

I had taken the subway at unsocial hours before but I had never seen it as empty as it was that night.

It was very quiet and there was no one else around, at least that's what I thought until I noticed someone standing behind one of the columns near the edge of the platform.

I leaned forward to get a better look but it almost felt like the stranger was intentionally trying to avoid being seen, so I just looked straight ahead and minded my own business.

The silence didn't last long after that. Suddenly, I could hear the sound of someone whistling. It appeared to come from all directions and there was something about it that made me feel uneasy.

Luckily, it was soon overshadowed by the sound of a train fast approaching.

As I prepared to embark on the train I was surprised to see a well-dressed man step out from behind the column and walk to the edge of the platform.

I felt relieved to see that it wasn't some thug or potential trouble maker yet still, something was strangely off about him and he seemed somewhat gaunt.

It always made me feel a little nervous to see someone standing so close to the edge of the platform, even when it was a stranger but I suspected he was just as anxious to get to his destination as I was. Midnight was close upon us after all.

He stood there very still and hadn't acknowledged my presence whatsoever until he slowly started turning his head towards me.

With eyes wide open, he greeted me with a creepy grin and an unsettling stare. I made a conscious effort to ignore him staring at me like that, but then he employed a sinister laugh which was then followed by something that still horrifies me to this day.

As the train made its way along the station platform the man just casually stepped directly into its path. I rushed to try to save him, but it was too late.

It took me a few seconds to grasp what I had just seen and I was still in shock when I hurried to the nearest ticket booth to get help. This resulted in an entire shut down of the subway.

The subway employees inspected both the track and the train but they didn't find any evidence of a body or even a single drop of blood.

After checking the tunnels, their attention shifted to me and the tone of the whole situation took a drastic turn for the worse.

I implored them to check the cameras to prove that I wasn't lying, but when they reviewed the footage, there was no sign of the man. It was just footage of me running towards an oncoming train.

I could see myself in the video playback…it was me alright. I ran towards the train and then stopped just in time to avoid getting hit.

My parents were told what happened and rumors spread very quickly after that.

As a devoted catholic, my mother never looked at me the same way again and my father just put on a brave face.

When that happened, the truth didn't really matter that much anymore, and life sort of carried on without ever really going back to normal.

I left home the same year and moved into a shabby old apartment downtown.

Needless to say, commuting around the city never felt quite the same after that, and I still find myself staring at the ceiling every night contemplating the truth about what I witnessed that fateful day at the subway.

Story 7

They Move On Their Own

I had just moved into a new apartment and had been living there for maybe two weeks before things started to get…weird.

The day started just like any other but things soon changed when I heard an unexpected knock on my door.

It was one of the other tenants from the floor below complaining about strange noises coming from my apartment and asking me to stop moving things around so late at night.

I was initially confused and told the neighbor that he was mistaken but nevertheless, he seemed convinced that the noise was coming from directly above his apartment.

A few days later, however, I did start noticing something strange. It was only little things at first. I noticed objects around the apartment that seemed out of place.

But I thought that perhaps I was just being forgetful and distracted. Things at work had been stressful lately so I had quite a lot of things on my mind.

But then something happened that I simply couldn't ignore.

I don't know how, but for some reason, the furniture in my apartment had been completely re-arranged while I was sleeping.

Nothing was missing and there were no signs of a break in.

I wasn't a very deep sleeper so I couldn't explain how all this happened without being woken up by the noise.

Then I heard another knock on the door. It was the neighbor from downstairs again.

This time he seemed a lot more agitated and I could tell his patience was running out. I didn't know what to say, but he threatened to submit an official complaint to the building owner if I didn't stop.

Things were getting worse and I needed to get to the bottom of it. The last thing I needed was to get evicted so I decided to make the most of the weekend to investigate further.

I quietly moved the furniture back into place, made sure my front door was locked and I set up my phone to record any audio while I was sleeping in the hopes that it might provide some clues to what was going on.

The next morning, I woke up and saw that once again, all of the furniture had been re-arranged in exactly the same way as before.

On the one side, I was fearful of what was going on but I was also hopeful that my phone picked up something that might reveal the truth.

I could only sit in silence and disbelief as I played back the audio.

What I heard was light footsteps that seem to come from all directions. Sometimes they sounded like someone was tiptoeing in the room and other times it sounded like multiple people were running around the apartment.

As well as the footsteps, there was the sound of furniture being dragged around the room. But what really chilled my blood was the faint breathing throughout the whole audio.

I still couldn't understand how I was not awoken by these noises. Even the neighbor from downstairs could hear it. The thought of having a stranger in my apartment moving things around while I slept was extremely unsettling.

If I was going to go to the police, I knew I needed some solid proof so I decided to set up a camera and leave it recording. This would undoubtedly reveal the truth, no matter how terrifying.

Strangely enough, I found myself almost getting used to the idea of finding my furniture in a different place every morning but now I had what I needed.

I hooked up my camera to my notebook and began scanning over the footage. What I witnessed next, was something truly horrifying.

The footage was dark and grainy but I could clearly see human form shadows darting around the room. I could clearly see shadows…but no one was in the room.

The video also showed my furniture moving around the room…on their own.

After reviewing the footage, I felt so lost and completely alone. With nowhere else to stay and no one to turn to, I decided to spend the next few nights in my car.

Whatever was going on in that room while I slept was too creepy for me to even think about sticking around. A week or so later I managed to find another apartment.

After settling in to my new apartment I decided to take another look at the footage I had taken. I found the file on my notebook and pressed play. The footage showed nothing but a blank grey, grainy background. No sound and no evidence.

At that moment I heard a knock at the door. It was my new neighbor from downstairs. She didn't look happy at all. She said that she had a very important meeting today and was late because she overslept.

She told me the next time I decide to move heavy furniture around my apartment that I should at least have the decency to do it during the day.

Story 8

Grinning Revenge

When I was a sophomore in high school I joined the basketball team. Although I made the team I rarely got to play. I was not very tall but I was a really good free-throw shooter so I was only used when needed.

In order to make sure I didn't get rusty I would often stay behind at school to get regular practice. Many times I ended up being one of the last people to leave the school building.

One Friday in early December I was at school rather late practicing. I needed to refill my water bottle so I walked out of the gym and down the hallway.

Along the way, I noticed that somebody was standing outside the school double doors. When he saw me he started frantically banging on the door. I wasn't allowed to let anybody into the building but this guy just kept banging trying to get my attention.

I walked over to the window and I let him know I couldn't let him in. He told me he was a school janitor and that he had left his keys inside his office and he begged me to let him inside.

I just shrugged at him and let him know I couldn't let him in and walked away. However, he just ignored what I had told him and kept banging on the doors.

I filled my water bottle up and walked back to the gym. This guy was still there banging on the doors trying to get my attention.

I figured the best thing to do was just ignore him, so I didn't acknowledge him the second time. This just made him really angry though and he actually called me a few expletives as he walked away.

Anyway, I walked back into the gym to continue my monotonous routine of free throwing. I had gone through about 20 straight hits when I finally missed one and the ball bounced off the hoop and rolled over to the double doors.

As I walked over to it I noticed it was now snowing pretty hard outside. I decided to call it a day and just walk home before the snow got too bad. I reached down to pick up the ball and when I stood up I was face to face with the "crazy" guy again.

He didn't say anything to me this time…he just looked at me in the eyes for what seemed to be an eternity. Then the corner of his mouth curved up to reveal a creepy half smile.

He grabbed the door handle and pulled on it. Of course he didn't get in but he certainly made sure to noisily rattle the doors.

His eyes never left mine. He must have known that he had shaken me up a bit because his half smile now became an evil looking full smile. He then turned and left.

I decided not to go home right away. I thought it'd be better just to waste some time in the gym and wait for the guy to get bored and leave or something.

I wasn't really worried about getting home in the snow because I didn't live very far from the school. I practiced for about another hour and a half and then finally decided it was time to go home.

It was snowing pretty hard by the time I left the school building. I stood at the door for a good twenty minutes waiting to see if the man was still out there. Obviously I'd angered him but it's not like I did anything wrong.

Still, even an angry guy probably wouldn't spend nearly two hours in a fierce snowstorm just to kick my ass. That would be really freaky.

I began walking home. It was dark and the snow was falling at a fairly fast rate. It didn't take long before my shoes were completely soaked and I almost cursed myself for waiting so long to go home.

Suddenly, someone grabbed me from behind knocking me face-first onto the ground. I fell forward hard and got snow my eyes and dropped my backpack.

When I finally was able to get the snow out of my eyes I turned around and saw the guy from earlier standing behind me with my backpack in his hand.

I was scared to death at first, thinking he was going to beat the crap out of me for not helping him out earlier. Nothing happened though, he simply stood there in the snow not moving.

Then he put his hand out to offer to help me up. I was cautious to accept it but I finally did. He helped me back up and then just handed me my backpack. The whole time not saying a word and just staring right at me with that creepy half smile again.

I reached out and grabbed my backpack and tried to pull it over to me. At first he held on tightly to it but after a few seconds he released his grip.

I took my backpack and nervously thanked him for helping me up. He of course did not respond…just smiled at me.

I turned and began to walk home but I kept watching him as I walked away completely expecting him to rush me. He didn't do anything, he didn't even slowly follow me, he just stood there watching me as I walked away.

Thank God by the time I got to my house the man was nowhere to be seen. My parents were home and I felt completely safe.

I got cleaned up, had a nice dinner with them and by the time my parents had went to bed I had nearly forgotten about the encounter with the weird guy.

I decided to do a little bit of homework before bedtime so I went to my room and over to my desk. I got my backpack and opened it up. I reached in to grab my notebooks and noticed they were all wet. I was angry at myself for getting snow in my bag, however when I pulled out one of my books I realized that it wasn't wet with melted snow…it was wet with blood.

Freaked out, I dropped my bag to the floor. Once I had composed myself I grabbed the bag by the bottom and dumped the contents onto the floor.

Along with my books, pencils and notebooks half a body of what appeared to be a Yorkshire Terrier fell out onto the floor. It looked like it was cut in half. The top half of its lifeless body just stared at me with dead black eyes.

Story 9

Bath time horror

I was home alone one evening. The rest of my family had gone out to do something that I didn't really care for, so I decided not to join them.

Once they left, I thought it'd be a good time to enjoy a nice solitary bath. As I ran the bath I decided it would be a good idea to let my dog out in the yard as she needed to go out. I then went to my bedroom closet to get a towel to dry off with after my bath.

Suddenly, I heard my dog barking like crazy outside. I assumed she was barking at a squirrel or something like that so I didn't really take much notice.

After another minute or two of her barking like that I decided she probably wanted to come back into the house. So, I let her back inside making sure I closed and locked the door.

I turned off the porch light and then crawled into my bath for a nice soak. As I sat in the bathtub I thought about my dog's barking; there was something about the entire situation that gave me a bad vibe.

The back door to the house, where I let the dog out, has an incredibly loud creak when opened. You can hear its creaking sound throughout the entire house, even from behind closed doors.

As I begin to relax and sink into the tub I hear the door creak open very slowly. I immediately go numb as thoughts raced through my head.

Is this really happening? I think someone is breaking into my home! Then seconds later I hear footsteps coming up the first flight of stairs.

I quickly hopped out of the bathtub, locked the bathroom door and turned off the lights. I was now in the corner of the room, in the dark and absolutely terrified.

The footsteps on the stairs disappeared, but only for a few moments. When the sounds returned, they were right on the other side of my bathroom door.

My heart pounded in fear as I stared at the door knob. It began to slowly turn.

At this point I did everything I could to not scream or make any other noises. I sat there curled up in the corner with my hands covering my mouth…listening intently.

I was wishing that whoever was on the other side of that door would eventually go away. To my immense relief I could hear the footsteps go back downstairs.

I had survived! I was still panicking though. I told myself this wasn't actually happening and that if I went downstairs there'd be nothing there.

So I mustered up some courage and slowly opened the door. I peeked into the hallway and saw nothing unusual.

I then walked down the stairs fully expecting to see some burglar walk into my view. I looked at the back door and the door was completely closed and still locked.

That couldn't be! That's impossible! I was certain I had heard the door creak, just like I'd heard it a million times before. The only difference this time is it was long and slow…as if someone was trying their best not to be heard.

Something even scarier was the fact that I never heard the door creak a second time; which meant whoever was here never left the house!

I locked myself in my bedroom for the rest of the night and when my family came home I ran to them and told them everything that had happened.

They took me at my word and searched the entire house but of course no one was found. There was no sign that anyone had broken in.

Was it all my imagination? Was it the world's weirdest break-in? Or was it a spirit entering my home and deciding not to leave?

MORE BOOKS IN THE CREEPY STORY HOUR COLLECTION...

**Scary Short Stories for Teens
Book 1**

**Scary Short Stories for Teens
Book 2**

Printed in Great Britain
by Amazon